The Amazing Secret

Crossway books by Joni Eareckson Tada
I'll Be with You Always
You've Got a Friend

Joni Eareckson Tada and Steve Jensen
Tell Me the Promises
Tell Me the Truth

DARCY AND FRIENDS
The Amazing Secret
The Unforgettable Summer

The
Amazing Secret

JONI EARECKSON TADA
STEVE JENSEN

CROSSWAY BOOKS • WHEATON, ILLINOIS
A DIVISION OF GOOD NEWS PUBLISHERS

Cover design: Liita Forsyth

Cover illustration: Matthew Archambault

First printing 2000

Printed in the United States of America

Library of Congress Cataloging-in-Publication Data
Tada, Joni Eareckson.
  The amazing secret / Joni Eareckson Tada and Steve Jensen.
    p. cm. — (Darcy and Friends series)
  Summary: Feeling hopeless, Darcy, a young paraplegic, rejects the friendship of Eric, a burn victim with a severely disfigured face, who ultimately teaches Darcy about forgiveness.
  ISBN 1-58134-197-0
  [1. Physically handicapped—Fiction. 2. Forgiveness—Fiction. 3. Christian life—Fiction.] I. Jensen, Steve. II. Title.
PZ7.T116 Davk 2000
[Fic]—dc21   00-008985
                                      CIP

15	14	13	12	11	10	09	08	07	06	05	04	03	02	01	00
15	14	13	12	11	10	9	8	7	6	5	4	3	2	1	

To Jessi, Bethany, and Sarah—beautiful gifts from the Lord, who have learned to love Him and people with disabilities.

One

Two hundred forty-two, two-forty-three, two-forty-four . . .

I counted the tiny specks of color on the floor tile directly below me. I had started in the lower left corner of the eight-inch tile and had moved to the upper right corner. I was almost finished.

Two hundred forty-five, two-forty-six, two-forty-seven, two-forty-eight . . .

It had seemed an important thing to know when I first started. I had imagined that Willowbrook Hospital where I was staying might want to know. And certainly the company that made the tile would want to know. They could put it in an ad on TV or something—*"Our brand has 13 percent more specks than the other leading brand! Just ask Darcy!"*

According to my plan, if I knew how many specks were on one tile, I could multiply that number by the number of tiles in the room. Once I figured out how many specks were in this room, I could multiply that number by the number of rooms on this floor. I'd then figure out how many specks there were in the hallway and add that number in. And once I knew the number of specks on this floor, I'd multiply that number by the number of floors in the hospital—five. By the time I finished calculating, the number of specks would be in the billions or even gazillions!

"Two hundred forty-nine, two hundred fifty, two hundred fifty-one!" I counted the last three numbers out loud slowly and proudly. I would have been more excited if the number had ended with a zero. Multiplying would be so much easier if I had a round number like 900 or 1,000. No matter. I had just finished the hardest part of the job. I took a deep breath and started counting the tiles, moving from the left side of the room to the right.

Everything seemed to go according to plan until I reached the middle of the room. Then the loudspeaker blared, "Code 99," "Code 99." It was an emergency with a patient somewhere in the building. I completely lost my place in the count. I sighed. I would have to start over from the beginning.

Starting over, though, caused me to think about what I was doing. I could imagine the head nurse patting me on the head for a moment and saying, "Isn't that interesting," and then moving on down the hallway. And the tile company? *Get real*, I thought. *What a dumb commercial that would make!* What had seemed to be a challenge, something people would find amazing, now seemed a waste of time. No one would care. And neither did I. I stopped when I reached thirty-four tiles.

"This is stupid," I said aloud.

No one heard me. I was alone in a hospital room surrounded by blank white walls. There was nothing about the room that felt like "mine," except for a couple of family photos my mom had tacked on a bulletin board by the head of my bed. But at this point, I couldn't even see them. I was trapped in a bed turned upside down—a Stryker frame, they called it. It was a special bed made to turn people over on the stomach when they needed the weight of their body taken off the backside. My forehead rested on a cushion. An opening in the frame from my forehead down to my shoulders allowed me to look about the room below me.

Were it not for the fact that I had to stay in this bed for hours at a time each day, the sensation of hanging four feet off the floor might actually have been fun. There was nothing below me, and I had to trust that bed to hold me in place. Sometimes I'd read a book they placed on the floor. Occasionally, if I turned my head at a certain weird angle, I could almost see out the window in my room. Also there was a mirror angled toward the opposite wall and ceiling so that I could watch TV, but watching words on the screen spelled out backwards would get annoying after a while. Listening to CDs or sleeping were the only two activities I found to help pass the time. Or doing something stupid like counting specks on the floor.

It was the third, and hopefully final, week in the Stryker frame. The doctors were treating me for a sore on my hip that had grown through my skin over the summer. A pressure sore, they called it—something common for paralyzed people who have to sit for long periods of time but who can't feel what they're sitting on. It had begun as a harmless red spot on my skin. But the constant pressure of my bone against my muscle and skin from the inside began to take its toll.

The sore had first appeared in August. My mom usually kept a good eye on me, but things had been hectic around our house near the end of school. I had visited my aunt for two months on her farm. The ground and driveway on the farm were bumpy, causing my hip bone to jostle hard against my flesh. To make things worse, I had taken my old wheelchair with me, one that didn't fit as well and pinched my body in places that my new one didn't. My skin finally gave up.

Though my mom tried her best, the sore grew each day. By the time she finally took me to the doctor in October, he said the sore had gotten deeper, almost to the bone. I was in bad shape. I couldn't stay at home and get better, they told me. I had to go into the hospital.

I had stayed on this same floor in Willowbrook Hospital four years ago when I was seven. A car had clipped the back end of my bike as I crossed the street. It sent me flying against the rear of a parked car. That broke the spinal cord that runs down the center of my back. I could no longer move or feel anything from my stomach all the way down to my toes. At Willowbrook, I learned how to do things—like how to move around in my wheelchair and change my clothes. I would learn to live as normally as possible.

Learning to do things encouraged me back then, but I honestly didn't feel like a normal girl at all right now. How many girls count specks on tiles while they hang for hours over the floor? How many have holes eating away at their skin? How many kids need to have their family lie on the floor in order to talk to them? How many have to watch TV backwards and upside down?

A huge sigh escaped me. I had become tired of being paralyzed. Tired of being left out of things. Tired of doctors. Tired of hearing my parents argue over money and stuff. Tired of everything. I closed my eyes to try and forget the hour I had just wasted. But the image of the tile was still there. The specks pulsed like stars in the darkness behind my eyelids. *This is all I'll ever see in my life—tiles, carpets, and floors.*

* * *

I was too embarrassed to cry out loud. I knew some nurse would give me a pep talk on how it will all get better soon, and I'd be able to enjoy this or that and be just like any other girl. Or worse yet, someone would play the army sergeant role: "Snap out of it!" "Quit complaining and grow up!" And then there would be the comedians who tried to make me laugh. "It's a new theory about getting better," they'd say. "Your body heals faster when you laugh." Ha, hah. I'm tied up like a pig on a barbecue roast, and they're talking about making me laugh.

I would not cry out loud, but I would cry. I let the tears spill quietly. They slowly rolled down my cheeks and dropped easily to the floor directly below me. I watched them splatter and then collect into small puddles, magnifying the specks underneath. I was fascinated by the effect—so fascinated I didn't notice the shadow that had entered the room and parked itself to my left.

"What are ya doing?" he asked. The shadow wore khakis and had a boy's voice.

I snuffled in loudly through my nose when I heard him. I was embarrassed and angry. "What?" I snapped back.

"I said, 'What are you doing?'" the voice replied calmly.

"What kind of stupid question is that?"

"I don't know. You must be laying upside down for a reason, so I thought I'd ask. Didn't know it would ruin your day." He turned away, his sneakers squeaking on the floor. He nearly reached the door before I realized he hadn't deserved my anger.

I called out, "Hey, wait a minute!"

He stopped. "Yeah?"

"I'm sorry. I didn't mean to—uh—come back. I mean, if you're not doing anything, I—uh—need some help." I was embarrassed, but I really needed someone's help to clean up my nose from crying. I was such a mess I didn't care who saw me. Or who cleaned up after me.

He walked back slowly. "What do you need?"

"A tissue. My face needs some wiping up. Would you mind?"

I heard him move about the room, lifting things here and there. He returned shortly.

"No tissue, but there was a small towel."

"Just put it below my face, okay? I'll do the work." I buried my face in the towel. I almost burst into tears again, but I held back. It wouldn't do any good to cry more.

"So why *are* you here?" he asked when I finished.

I answered politely, "I've got a pressure sore on my hip from sitting on it too long. I lie on this thing so my hip has a chance to heal."

"So . . . like you're a real pain in the—"

"Hah, hah," I interrupted. "A real comedian." I paused. "I wish it were a pain. At least I'd feel it. I can't though. And I can't move either. I'm paralyzed from my waist down."

"Oh. So how long do you have to lay like this?"

I got sarcastic again. "When you stop asking questions probably!"

The shadow just laughed back at me, sounding a bit annoyed himself. "So who licked the icing off your cupcake this morning?"

I burst into laughter. "Good one. Where'd you hear that?"

"On TV. There's a lot of TV-watching going on around here."

"Yeah, tell me about it. Are you a patient here? How long have you been in this place?"

"Well, I'm kind of like a patient, I guess. I've been here a lot."

We changed the subject and moved on to discussing the latest TV shows we had seen. He talked a lot about one on the space program. He told me all about the rockets, the sizes of the shuttles, the speed of the orbiters on the way to Mars. I had never been into rockets, but he made them sound interesting. There was something about his voice that made me want to listen. It wasn't a nice voice particularly. But he ended each sentence on a higher note, as if discovering the words that he had just formed and finding delight in them.

"Everything all right in here, you two?" A nurse interrupted our conversation. "How are you doing, Eric?"

"Fine, thanks."

Eric. We had spent nearly an hour together, and I only now learned his name. "I'm Darcy," I said.

"It's time to flip, Darcy," the nurse continued. "The ceiling's been missing you."

Eric stepped away from the bed as the nurse undid a latch and turned me over. I spun around at what felt like four Gs on a jet plane. The room whirled before my eyes until the bed frame crashed into place. I felt dizzy for a few moments. The fluorescent lights blinded me.

The nurse tucked my sheets back into place as I searched for Eric. I wanted to see what this shadow and this voice looked like. It was the first person I had talked to in a long time that didn't talk about my body. And he didn't spend his time trying to make me feel better either. He just talked—talked the way friends would talk. I hoped we could be friends. Maybe the rest of my time in the hospital wouldn't be so bad. Maybe we'd hang out together and do stuff. Maybe he was cute. Maybe he . . .

My eyes adjusted to the glare of the sun streaming in from the window. The nurse moved away so that I had a clear vision of Eric. I was not prepared for what I saw.

mark out their place on his face. There were no eye-lashes to soften his gaze. All he had were his eyes, hid-den in the midst of a pain-marked face.

My gaze into his eyes lingered long, long enough to put him at ease that I would not be afraid or look away. His looked deep into mine as I studied him.

At last he spoke. "Hi. It's me, Eric. I'm also known as the mutant slug from the planet Izor. Live long and prosper." He held up his three-fingered hand and made a V sign like on *Star Trek*.

"Hi," I said weakly. My voice cracked a bit as I laughed at his joke. I was nervous, as if talking to a boy I liked in the lunch line at school.

The nurse continued working around my Stryker frame, folding towels and stuff. Sensing the conversation had come to a dead stop, she said, "I see you two know each other."

"Kind of," I said. "He came in a little while ago. I was . . ." I stopped, remembering my pity party. I didn't want the nurse to know I had been crying. I was sure she would make a speech about being thankful. I just wasn't in the mood.

"She was singing," Eric interrupted. I looked at him as if he had lost his mind. He shrugged his shoul-ders, apologizing for the obviously lame excuse. "Yeah,

you know," he continued with the white lie, "she was singing that hospital song about how bad the food is here and how the doctors wake you up at all hours of the night."

"Yes, and you would know, wouldn't you, Eric," the nurse played along. "You've been at this hospital longer than anyone. At least you used to be."

"Used to?" I asked.

"Oh, yeah. Eric here was a long-timer. Came in one day all burned up and then decided he'd like to stay awhile. How long was it—a year?"

"Thirteen months," Eric said proudly. "Had a birthday and Christmas here. And watched all four seasons go by. Missed a whole year of school, too."

The nurse kidded around more with Eric. It was obvious they were old friends. "Eric's friends with everybody around here," she said.

I went back to watching Eric again. He seemed relaxed, natural. But his face was so hard to look at. And yet I couldn't stop looking at it either. I just couldn't help but stare. The nurse caught me. "Well! Looks like it's time for your physical therapy," she said a little forcefully as the PT (that's short for physical therapist) walked into the room.

"So, Darcy, are you ready for your exercises?" the PT said.

I groaned. It was as if the two of them were punishing me for staring. I closed my eyes and did not respond. The PT directed Eric to leave. "Come back in about half an hour, Eric. I'll be finished taking your friend's bones apart by then!" She laughed, imitating an evil professor. She knew full well how painful it was and tried to lighten it up a bit.

"No pain, no gain." Eric joined in her attempt as he walked toward the door.

"Some friend you are!" I snapped back. I took advantage of the moment to call him a friend, even if it was in jest. "I bet you *are* one of them—one of those mutant slugs from the planet Azor!"

"It's Izor, Darcy. Izor. And, yes, I am one of them. Live long and prosper!" He shot a V through the door as he closed it behind him and then left.

❊ ❊ ❊

The half hour with the PT was filled with pain. And no gain. The exercises were supposed to help my blood circulate and to keep my muscles firm. All they did was make me sweat and cry. She moved my legs up and down, turning them in a circle into my hips. I felt like kicking her even though I couldn't. Although I was paralyzed, my body responded as if it could feel everything. My skin got hot, my breath short. And I got that same feeling in my stomach that you get when you hurt yourself badly. I felt like throwing up.

The PT stopped in time. "Okay, time's up. I know you want me to keep going, but we'll have to stop there." She knew I was on the verge of tears as well, and she smiled softly at me. "Time to change the dressing on your sore."

I loved and hated this part of the day. I loved it because I somehow believed that overnight the sore would heal up, and they'd tell me what a miracle it was and then send me home. And I hated this part because every day they'd say the same thing: "Well, it's getting there, Darcy. Just be patient. You're doing great."

This time I got a surprise. After the physical therapist took a look at my sore, she said, "I think it's time we took you off this Stryker frame."

I couldn't believe it. One of the aides rolled a bed into my room and angled it next to my Stryker frame. Within minutes they had lifted me out of that old torture rack and into the new bed. "Hey, this is an improvement!" I smiled. My smile didn't last long.

"Darcy, I'm afraid it's still going to take several more weeks to heal that sore of yours," the PT said as she hung my chart on the end of my new bed.

I rolled my eyes and groaned, "Oh, no!"

"Sorry," she added. "But it'll be one more week in the hospital to be sure the infection is gone and then several more weeks at home for the sore to heal."

As my PT left, a nurse carrying a washcloth and bath basin passed her in the doorway. "Hey, nice going," she said as she put down her things. "They've got you in a regular bed!"

"A *hospital* bed," I said under my breath. I tried to cover up my disappointment as I watched the nurse get things ready for my bath. I never admitted it, but I always looked forward to these baths. The warmth of the cloth and the tenderness of the nurse helped me to feel at ease. I decided that even the bed felt a little—no, a lot—better than that old Stryker frame. I closed my eyes and soon drifted off into a warm sleep.

✻ ✻ ✻

My hospital room was dark except for the light coming in from the hallway when I woke up. I adjusted my eyes to the darkness to find Eric sitting on the end of my bed. He walked over to the lamp across the room and turned it on, casting a warm glow in the room.

"Nice nap on this here new bed?" Eric asked as he patted the sheet.

"Hmm," I said. "What time is it?"

"Three hours after you first stared at me."

I blushed and turned away. "I'm sorry," I said. "I didn't mean to."

"That's okay. You're not the first person that's done that." Eric was smiling gently when I turned back to look at him. "I do kinda look like a mutant alien, don't I?"

"No, you don't! You look fine. Well, I mean, it doesn't look great, but it's not bad really." I was embarrassed still and not explaining myself real well.

Eric changed the subject for me. "So you're paralyzed."

"Yeah, I'm a paraplegic. Can't move from my waist down."

"How did it happen?"

It was at this point in the conversation with most people that I would begin to get uncomfortable and say something short: "A car hit me." Or I'd let my mom or dad interrupt and tell the story. They seemed to enjoy telling it and added stuff from their point of view. But when I looked at Eric, it was obvious that he was expecting more than that. He sat on the bed as if waiting to hear a campfire story. He balanced his elbows on his knees and rested his chin on his hands.

"It's a long story," I said, hoping to change his mind.

"I've got time," he answered. His eyes meant it. He would listen. I breathed deeply and told the whole story from my point of view.

❄ ❄ ❄

It was a cool afternoon in spring, and I remember the details as if it were yesterday. I had just come home from school, plopped my books on the kitchen table, and raided the fridge. Halfway through my glass of chocolate milk, I noticed I had left the kitchen door open. The spring air felt so new and fresh that I decided I would go back out and play.

That was when I heard Chip and Mandy call me from outside on their bikes. I threw on a sweatshirt, darted out the door, and pedaled my bike down our driveway. A few minutes later we were circling our bikes around at the end of my street, going up and down the driveways.

We had made up a new game the week before using the sidewalk as a runway for a make-believe airport. The driveway at Chip's house at the end of the block was where we took off. My house was the terminal where people got on the planes. We'd line up one at a time waiting for our planes to get fuel, and then we would take off down the runway. When we got to Chip's driveway, we went down toward the street and then up the edge of the curb. It would make the front of our bikes tilt up into the air, and for just a second we'd be flying through the air. When we came down, we would head across the street and back down the opposite sidewalk and then "land" our bikes back at my house.

We had done this several times that afternoon. Sometimes two of us would fly at the same time. It seemed really cool to us seven-year-olds to do something we had seen older kids do at school. Soon we were timing ourselves with Chip's stopwatch that his dad had given him.

"Let's keep time to see how fast we can make the whole trip around the block," Chip suggested. We lined up one by one, eager to be the fastest "plane." I was fourth in line. Chip was the last one behind me, keeping time.

Each kid took a turn racing down the sidewalk as fast as he or she could go. Mike was the first. He did it in forty-three seconds. Then Mandy did it in thirty-eight seconds. Jennifer did it in fifty-five seconds. I laughed at her for being so slow. "Watch me, and I'll show you how to do it!" I jeered. Jennifer was a little on the heavy side and always slow at games.

I took off down the sidewalk at the sound of Chip's "Go!" My legs pumped so fast that the bicycle pedals couldn't keep up with me. The sidewalk and bushes rushed by at incredible speed. The wind was behind my back, pushing me even faster. I could hear the kids yelling from behind, cheering me on. The launching point was just a short ways ahead, and I gripped the handles hard, waiting for the moment when I would have to yank up on the handle bar, steer through the air, and then land without falling. I was one of the best at doing this, and I believed my time would be the fastest that day. The cheers got louder. I gripped harder. I pedaled furiously for the last ten feet.

I hit the edge of the curb just right. I pulled back

on the handle bars at just the right moment. The back wheel and the front wheel were at a perfect angle. The sun was low in the sky at the end of the street. A warm breeze picked up just as I hit the top of the arc of my flight. And the landing was perfect—back wheel first, then the front. Both were straight. I began pedaling as soon as I could. I heard more cheers behind me as I turned toward the opposite side of the street.

It was at that point that my life changed completely. Though some people say that they can't remember what happened to them in an accident, I remembered it as clearly as I remembered the thrill of flying. I can still hear, see, feel, and smell everything from those few moments.

As I was halfway across the street, I heard a horn honk from my left. I saw it at the same time, almost. It was a sports car. A red Corvette convertible. I remember it was a convertible because in the passenger seat was a girl with long blonde hair blowing up into the wind. I slammed on my brakes at the same time that the driver of the car hit his. I probably would have made it safely across if I hadn't tried to stop. But it was instinct, something you do naturally when you see a big red sports car come straight at you.

The car didn't hit me directly but instead hit my back wheel. That caused my bike to spin around. I was thrown about fifteen feet before crashing into the back of a parked van. I was flying sideways at that point, so my back hit the corner of the van. My head hit the side, and then I fell to the ground beside the van. I remember smelling the asphalt before a terrible pain shot through my entire body. My arm was buckled underneath me, causing me more pain than any other part of my body. They said blood was coming from my head and that I looked like I ought to be dead. I wasn't. There was too much pain to be dead. I screamed.

I remembered everything, including the scared look on the face of the guy driving the red sports car. He shoved it into gear and sped away, making his tires squeal and leaving a trail of smoke behind him. I remember Chip kneeling over me, asking if I was okay. I moaned. I was surprised when I heard my mom's voice. She ran to me from across the street and then yelled back at my older sister to call the ambulance. A crowd of neighbors began to gather, and I started to cry a little. I was scared all during the ambulance ride to the hospital with my mom.

✳ ✳ ✳

"And that's what happened," I finished. I looked up at Eric.

Eric nodded. "Wow! Pretty nasty. And so you're still mad about it, huh?"

I hadn't shared my feelings about the accident. Where did Eric get the nerve to say I was angry?

"What do you mean?" I asked with an edge to my voice.

"I don't know. You just seem angry about it, that's all."

"I'm not angry about it," I insisted. Eric stared at me with his eyes. He wasn't convinced.

"I'm not angry!" I said loudly. This time I really was mad. Mad at Eric. I had just unloaded a painful story for the first time to someone, and he had the nerve to sit there and tell me I was angry. "Who do you think you are?" My voice began to rise. "What are you, some kind of doctor?"

Eric was silent. He moved off the bed, glancing my way a little before walking toward the door. "I'm sorry.

I just thought you might want to talk about it. Someone helped me once and . . ."

I snapped my head around and faced the opposite wall. He stopped talking then and left the room completely. The room darkened as he pulled the door closed behind him.

Three

The next day gray clouds blew in to match my dark mood. A hard and heavy rain blustered outside my room, forming a sheet of running water that covered the window. The trees and buildings outside were barely visible. I felt as if I were trapped inside a car wash, unable to escape the noise and water.

There was no escape from myself either. My emotions and thoughts ran in circles, following no logical path. Like the driving raindrops against the window, my thoughts drove hard against my heart.

Why do I even care what Eric thinks anyway? What is he, some psychologist or something? Where does he get the idea that he can just sit on my bed and start getting nosy? I had wanted him to stay, but he had no right to say what he did. *He doesn't know what it feels like to be in a wheelchair, unable to move or feel anything.*

And what would he be able to do about my life anyway? He didn't live in my family or have to put up with stuff I had to go through. I thought about my family and what it had been like since my accident. It seemed that everything in our life had to do with me being paralyzed. We had to buy a special van with a lift. We had to add a ramp going into our house so I could get in and out. Dad changed the entire bathroom around just for me. Even our vacation plans had to revolve around me. Would the motel have the right kind of room? Were the trails in the park good enough for a wheelchair? Did the camp have the right kind of bed?

Not that we could take very many vacations. It seemed like Dad and Mom were always arguing about money. Dad wouldn't let Mom go out and get a job because he wanted her to stay at home. That meant he got a second job, coming home late at night and usually crabby. The doctor bills were always way higher than whatever money they made. That meant everyone had to give up stuff they wanted. My sister Monica and my brother Josh usually got secondhand clothes at the thrift shop. This was especially hard on Monica who had always been a real clothes horse. She had to work to pay for everything she wanted. Josh didn't get an allowance, and asking for stuff his friends had was always a hassle. The two of them never said anything, but I could tell they blamed me.

They might as well have blamed me, too, for how our life at church ended up. We used to have a blast at church and would go for everything. But after my accident, it became too much work. I also overheard Mom say once that people treated her differently, as if there was something wrong. I'm not sure what she meant, but I do know there was one lady Mom avoided all the time. The lady told Mom once that I had the accident because there was something that my mom or dad did that God wasn't happy about. Or it might have even been something I did. Anyway, the lady said my mom needed to confess her sin. Mom didn't go to church as much after that, although it seemed like she got closer to God somehow.

People at church prayed a lot when I first had my accident. I remember them coming to my hospital room all the time. And they were always real helpful. They'd bring over food almost every night, Josh told me. "Some of it's gross, but some of it's really good. Mom says it sure beats microwave dinners!" And there were always people cleaning and helping with other chores, my mom told me. It continued after I got out of the hospital for a couple of weeks. It stopped after that. I guess people figured I was as normal as I was ever going to be, and there wasn't a big emergency anymore.

There were lots of people like that—people who would come into our lives for a short time. I remember one man showed up at our house and said he was there to heal me. My mom and dad didn't know what to think. I mean, we all wanted me to be healed, but he said it as if we were stupid for not wanting it to happen. He said we just had to have enough faith. He came into our living room and put his hand on my head and started praying. When I didn't move after he first ended his prayer, he started praying again. Then he told me to pray hard, and he asked everyone to gather around and pray together. "You can't pray without faith!" he nearly yelled at us after the second time he prayed. He asked each one of us to pray. When that didn't make a difference, he told us that we were stubborn and not listening to God's will. He tried to blame us, I think. *If God wants me to be healed, I thought, he might as well do it and get it over with.* God didn't need this man yelling at me and my family in order for me to be healed.

* * *

The last four years had been like that, filled with times of being frustrated, lonely, and hurt. I stared at the rain beating against my window.

God, I know You're real, and I know You know every-thing. But this isn't fair. Why do I have to live life like this? It was okay when I was younger. It was kinda cool having my own wheelchair and our own van. I'd get to be the first one in line at amusement parks, and I'd usually end up in the newspaper on holidays and stuff. But I'm done with that now. I don't want to be in this bed any-more, in this hospital. I don't want to use a wheelchair. I don't want to be different. I want to run and walk like everyone else. I want to have feet that don't look all puffed up. I want to stub my toe and feel it. I want to put on clothes that look cool. I want to . . .

I'd done this before, making a list of things I wanted to do. It would make me feel better for a little while, but it didn't change anything. It was hopeless. And feeling hopeless made me tired. I cried deeply for the second time. Then I fell asleep.

* * *

It was either my mom's voice or the bright sun that woke me up the next morning. I had slept soundly, not remembering that I had been awakened three times during the night in order to be turned onto a different side. I usually stayed awake for a while after they turned me, but last night I must have been too exhausted to notice.

"So, dear, how did you sleep?" my mom asked. She wore a bright blue turtleneck and a pair of jeans with boots. A heart pendant hung from a gold chain around her neck. She sat down beside me and stroked my hair.

"Fine," I said, as I rubbed my eyes and squinted against the bright sunshine.

She noticed and moved to close the shades. "Well, I talked to the doctor today. He said you can start getting into your wheelchair for a couple of hours each day. And . . . he thinks you might be out of here before Thanksgiving. Wouldn't that be great?"

"Yeah, great," I said. "You can take me home Thanksgiving and stuff me as the turkey."

Mom couldn't tell if I was joking or being sarcastic. "You all right this morning? Anything bothering you?"

I shook my head. She walked back and stood next to me. "I've got to go down to the school and work things out with your teacher. You've gotten some work done here at the hospital, but she says you're falling behind a bit. Shouldn't be a problem, she said, but we need to talk." She looked at me with the smile she used when she was worried—all lips, no teeth.

I didn't answer her but rather took her worry and added it to the list of things I didn't like about me and my world. I just nodded, and she responded with a kiss on my forehead and a promise to come see me at lunchtime with more schoolwork. I watched her leave. "I'll stay longer next time, Darcy," she said as she stuck her head back through the doorway. "Really."

"Sure, Mom," I said, putting on a brave face. "See you later."

I started crying before her shadow left the doorway. It wasn't that she was leaving me. We had done this a hundred times before. It was just that this morning I wanted her to stay, to make it all better, to tell me that she really knew how things would turn out. I cried easily. The tears flowed down both sides of my cheeks. My eyes stung. My nose began to clog. I was turning into a mess again, but I didn't care. This time I'd let it all out. This time I'd—

"Hi! How ya doin'?"

Eric burst through the doorway as if there were a fire in the building. "Wanna do something?"

I snapped my head away from where he stood, not wanting him to catch me crying again. Yesterday was okay. He was a stranger then. And crying happens to all of us at one point or another. But this time I didn't want him to know how I felt. He had already intruded on my feelings once.

I kept silent, staring at the wall beside me.

"Ah, do you want to join some of the others in the Activity Room? I heard the nurse say you could get into your wheelchair now."

I didn't answer.

"We're gonna organize a Thanksgiving play. Little kids from the cancer ward will be there. They need some help with making their Indian and Pilgrim cos- tumes. I'm going as a turkey. How about you?"

I still did not answer or look in his direction.

"Oh, I get it," he said. "You want to go as Plymouth Rock, right? Get it? A rock—doesn't say much. Just lies there?"

I smiled inside at the joke, but I was in no mood to give him any satisfaction.

"Ooh, you're tough. I can see this is going to take

drastic measures." I saw him pick up the clipboard at the end of my bed. "Doctor," he said in a foreign accent, "ve have ein grosse problema here. This girl ist gone crazy because she has got neinen humor—"

I stopped the stupid-doctor routine in mid-sentence with an explosion of words: "Get out! Get out of here, you annoying jerk! Who asked you to come in here anyway? Don't you have any manners? And stop trying to cheer me up! Don't you see I don't want your pity!"

I unloaded everything I felt and everything I had ever heard people say on TV when they were mad. I hardly knew what was coming out of my mouth. "I'm not some patient you can try to heal. Go out and heal yourself!"

The last words finally hit their mark. His grotesque smile left his face, and his eyes looked down at the floor. "I'm sorry," he said quietly. "I wasn't trying to do anything. . . . I . . . ." He stopped, unsure of what he really was trying to say. "I just saw you needing a friend yesterday, that's all. If that's not what you want, then fine. Just say so. You don't have to yell at me."

I looked directly at him, still angry with him but also upset with myself for saying the things I did. It made me hate myself all the more. "I'm sorry, too. Just go, okay?" I said.

He turned and walked out the door. His shoulders were slumped, and his hands were tucked deep into his pockets. He bumped into the nurse as she entered my room. She took a quick look at him and then over at me.

"Hmm. You two break up?" she laughed.

I stared at her, my eyes still wet and red from crying.

"Oh. Sorry," she said. "This isn't about you and Eric, is it?"

I turned away from her.

"Anything I can do to help?"

I spoke quietly. "Just get me out of here, that's all."

"Wish I could, sweetie, wish I could. But as long as you're in here—"

"Yeah, I know, 'make the most of it.'"

She laughed quietly and sat leaning against the large chair in the room. "Tired of hearing that, aren't you?"

I nodded.

"Don't blame you. But you know, you could take a lesson from Eric."

I began to give her a nasty look, but she held up her hand. "Seriously. Think about what he's been through. He's felt more pain in his life than you ever will. He was burned over most of his body, you know.

Spent a lot of time in this hospital. We were all proud of him when he left."

"Left? You mean he's not a patient here?" I asked.

"No, not really. He comes in once in a while to get a checkup, but most of the time he's here because he wants to be here."

"Why?"

"Oh, he just likes to walk around and talk to kids. Make them feel better. He does stuff with the little kids, too. He organizes stuff like games and things. Gets kids thinking about things other than themselves."

"But why?" I asked again.

"Because he . . . oh, I don't know. Just something he likes to do, I suppose. I've never really asked him."

"How old is he?"

"Thirteen or fourteen, I think."

"And what about his family? Does he have any brothers or sisters?"

"He used to have one of each. They died in the fire. So did his mom. It's just him and his dad now."

"What happened in the fire? How did it start?" I asked.

"Not sure, exactly. They said there was something suspicious about it. Something Eric did but that they couldn't prove. You'll have to ask him," she said as she gave me my supply of pills. "Down the hatch."

I took the four pills and swallowed quickly. "But if he's had so much pain and lost half his family, how come he seems happy?"

"Well . . ." She began forming her thoughts but stopped with a smile on her face. "You'll just have to ask him that yourself, too, I think." She finished marking my chart and left the room.

Four

I was left alone in the room with my curiosity about Eric growing by the minute. What had really happened with that fire? How would I ask him? Would he be upset? Try to hide the truth? And why would he come back here to this place? The hospital would be the last place I would come back to. Did he feel guilty? Was he forced to come back as some kind of punishment?

As if my questions summoned him, Eric stuck his head through the open doorway. "Hi," he said quietly. "Okay if I come in?"

I almost gushed out a string of apologies, but I paused instead and said quietly, "Sure."

Eric leaned down at eye level with me. He took his

hat off, exposing his bald head completely for the first time. "I'm sorry for earlier. I mean, I don't think I did anything wrong, but I feel bad that I upset you."

I didn't know what to say. I guessed this was an apology, but I was embarrassed that he was the one doing the apologizing.

My silence made him feel awkward. "Forgive me?" he asked.

I nodded, not really feeling any need to do so and not feeling anything but guilt. It made me all the more frustrated and angry with this guy who kept coming into my room. I felt like being rude again and telling him to leave, but he spoke first.

"Darcy, you have to come with me. We're going to do this Thanksgiving thing. It's a dumb play, I know, because I wrote it. But we need as many kids as possible in it. And I need older kids especially. Will you come? We're practicing downstairs right now!"

"Ah, I—"

"Great!" he interrupted, and went to get my wheelchair from the other corner of the room. He angled the chair next to the bed, helped me sit up, and then steadied it while I slid into it slowly. I had not been out of bed for three weeks, and I immediately felt dizzy.

"Are you okay?" he asked.

"Uh, yeah, I think so," I said weakly.

"Then let's get going!" Eric exclaimed and grabbed one handle with his good hand and began pushing.

"Hold on!" I snapped. "Let go of my chair!" I grabbed hold of the wheel rims, stopped the chair, and faced him. Having him push me like that was like touching my body. "Don't you *ever* touch my chair again! Do you understand?"

Eric nodded, stunned at the outburst and embarrassed for not understanding my feelings.

"It's okay," I said, breathing deeply and trying to get hold of myself. "Just . . . just stop it!" I said the words without knowing what I was saying.

"Stop what?"

"I don't know. Just stop trying to help me. I don't need your help. Now let's just go to your stupid play, and I'll be Plymouth Rock. Or an ear of corn. Whatever. Okay?"

"Whatever you say," Eric answered. He shook his head a bit and slumped his shoulders like a dog that had been whipped but did not know why. "Just follow me."

We left the room and went the entire length of the hallway, past opened doors to other rooms, past the nursing station. Eric hit the elevator button, and we waited in silence. I was grateful when the elevator doors opened, shut behind us, and then opened again in front of the activity room. There was lots of light and noise and color inside the room. It was a welcome relief.

"Hey, kids!" Eric yelled out. "Here's Darcy! She's going to be Plymouth Rock!" The dozen or so kids in the room, some in wheelchairs and some wearing bandages, all broke out in a cheer.

"Eric," I whispered loudly, "are you serious about this Plymouth Rock thing?"

"Yeah. Why?"

"How am I supposed to be a rock?"

"I don't know. Just sit there like you normally do." He laughed, and his smile made his grotesque face twist in an evil sort of way. "C'mon," he said before I could yell at him, "we've got work to do."

✤ ✤ ✤

The rest of the afternoon was spent "practicing" the play. It was the most chaotic, stupidest play about Thanksgiving I had ever seen. He had the Indians and Pilgrims doing a square dance. One of the Indians did a commercial for corn flakes cereal. The turkey and the Pilgrim's wife ended up becoming friends, and they served pizza for the main course. The actors were laughing more than they were acting. Through it all I sat quietly, annoyed at how long this disaster was taking to rehearse. I wanted to get out of there.

"Nice job on being a rock, Darcy," Eric finally said as he came near me. "We're done practicing. Wanna go for a walk?"

I resisted the temptation to make a funny joke about his question—me, walking? But I didn't resist making a comment about the play. "So you dragged me down here to be in this stupid play. Where did you find the script? In your little brother's kindergarten bag?"

The words came out before I remembered that his brother was dead. He just shrugged his shoulders. "Yeah, I guess it's pretty bad. But, hey, look at them. They love it!" He turned back to admire all the kids working on costumes and having a good time together. I had to admit he was right. And that annoyed me all the more.

"How about that walk?" he asked again.

"Okay," I said.

We left the Indians and Pilgrims behind and headed for the elevator.

"Let's go up to the roof!" Eric suggested as we got into the elevator. "It's really cool up there!"

"Cool? You bet it's cool. It's freezing. This is November, remember?"

"Yeah, but the rain's stopped, and the sun is out. We'll only be there a couple of minutes. C'mon. I've done it a hundred times. I'll show you my favorite spot."

We arrived at the fifth floor maternity ward where babies were born. The nurses' station was to the right of the elevator. We turned left down a small hallway after Eric checked to see that no one was looking in our direction. A door marked Exit and Authorized Personnel Only greeted us.

"Stay quiet," Eric said.

"But we're not supposed to go out there!" I whispered.

"Don't sweat it. I've been up here with doctors and nurses before. They come up here when they're on break and want to catch some sun. Trust me. It's okay."

"Then why are we whispering?" I asked.

Eric didn't answer. He looked back down the hallway to be sure the coast was clear and then opened the door. We entered a small room with four steps at the other end in front of the door that led to the roof. There might as well have been a hundred.

"Ah, no go, Eric," I said.

"What?"

"The stairs. I'm not getting out of my chair with these legs, and you're definitely not carrying me!"

Eric looked back and forth from my wheelchair to the stairs. "I've got an idea," he said. "There's some plywood outside on the roof. I'll bring it in and make a ramp, okay?"

He left without my answer and ran to the door. A cold wind and some light burst through as he opened it. "Whoa, it's cold out here!" he said as he disappeared onto the roof. The door closed behind him with a quiet click.

I sat in the small room alone. It was hardly a room, really. The floor was made of concrete. The walls were painted cinder blocks. The only light in the room was from an exit sign and from the gap below the door where the outside light came through. Within moments I became nervous. The unknown and the fact that I didn't think we were supposed to be doing this made me afraid. My teeth chattered. I nervously rubbed the pads on my wheelchair.

And then I heard voices.

They were real quiet at first, but they seemed to be coming in my direction. I tucked back into the corner and held my breath. The voices increased in volume and then became quiet as the bell to the elevator went "ding." I waited perfectly still.

Nothing.

Breathing out for the first time, I relaxed and rolled forward toward the door leading back to the main hallway. I pulled it open slowly and peaked toward the elevator. I then looked back toward the door to the roof. No Eric yet. I was getting more and more nervous about being caught. In an instant I made the decision to leave. Eric would catch up with me later and make fun of me, but I decided then and there that I wanted no part of his attempt to make me happy. Maybe this kind of stuff was cool for stories in *Reader's Digest*, but I wasn't in the mood to get caught. I hurried to the elevator and got on.

I returned to my room and got back into bed, nervous that I might have made my sore worse during the short time that I was away. My supper was waiting for me on a tray next to my bed—meatloaf, potatoes, and peas—and I began chowing it down. I glanced up and saw that the sky was turning darker again. The tops of the trees outside my window were bending and bouncing in the wind. It looked icy cold outside. Within minutes, the rain started spitting against the window pane, and then it turned into a downpour. A nurse's aide came into my room to pick up odds and ends.

"Pretty awful weather," she said, just to make conversation. We talked back and forth a little, but it was during my cherry Jell-O that her tone turned serious.

"By the way, have you seen Eric lately?"

"Ah . . . no. Why?" I lied, sort of. It was true I hadn't seen him for a while, but I didn't say when I had seen him last and where.

"Well, his dad called here a little while ago. Said Eric was supposed to be back in time for his piano lesson."

"Piano lesson? Eric?" I asked, wondering how a one-handed kid could play piano.

"Yeah. He's quite good, actually. He's played here at Christmas a couple of times. It's really amazing how he does it. Anyway, his dad knew he came here this morning to practice the play but expected him back right after that."

"Has anyone searched the building for him?"

"I suppose. You said you didn't see him, but you were at the practice, right?"

"Ah, yeah. I saw him there. He took me down there right after lunch."

I was beginning to sweat. The nurse looked at me as if I had something really important to say. I did, but I didn't get the chance to say it. At that moment the head nurse burst into the room. "Jenny, come quick! They found Eric! He was up on the roof. They've got him up in ICU now!"

Five

I waited to be sure that the hall outside my door was quiet before getting out of bed. I had to see Eric for myself. Why would he be in ICU anyway? What would being on the roof have to do with a life-and-death emergency? My head was full of all kinds of questions as I threw back my covers, reached for the arm of my wheelchair, and dragged it next to my bed. Within minutes I was out the door.

The big, heavy doors of ICU, short for the Intensive Care Unit, were directly ahead of me as I came out of the elevator. Every time a door swung open, I could see nurses and doctors moving about quietly but quickly. When two visitors came out, they held the door open for me like they thought I belonged in there. I took my chance and wheeled in. Nobody questioned me. One corner of ICU seemed especially busy, and I headed in that direction, going the long way around to avoid people. When I came to the alcove where I thought Eric might be, I tucked behind a desk and watched. Machines and tubes were everywhere, and a curtain was drawn halfway around the bed. People kept walking in and out of the alcove.

Someone shoved the curtain back, and I could barely make out a person in the bed. Just then I caught a glimpse of a hand at the end of an intravenous tube. It was Eric's. His normally dark skin was now grayish. I followed his arm up to his head, which was now clearly visible from where I hid. Eric had a tube going up his nose. He groaned and turned his head in my direction. I hoped he might see me, but his eyes were closed. Tears came to mine. I felt a wave of guilt wash over me. *It's not my fault*, I began to say to myself. I repeated it over and over in my head.

I don't know how long I sat there staring at Eric, but I was interrupted by a nurse shaking my shoulder.

"Are you supposed to be here?" she asked.

I looked up, tears brimming in my eyes. "I—I . . ."

"It's okay. You can stay," she said, seeing that I was upset. "Just stay parked right here where you're out of the way, okay?"

I nodded and asked, "What happened? Is he going to be all right?"

"Well, he might be. He's got a real high fever. Hard for him to breathe, too. He gets pneumonia easily on account of his lungs being damaged when he was in that fire. Just pray, honey. He'll need a lot of prayer."

"But what happened? How?"

"Hmm. It's the craziest thing. He was out on the roof of the building. Got caught in the rain apparently. We're not sure how long he was there, but a janitor found him right outside the door, huddled in the corner and unconscious. With the temperature as cold as it was and the rain and wind chill, I'm surprised he lived at all."

My heart sank, and I began to cry silently again. The tears flowed readily. I buried my face in my hands.

"Is he a good friend of yours?" the nurse asked.

"Kind of. He . . ." I didn't know how to answer. "He was helping me."

I was about to explain how Eric came to be on the roof, but a noise just outside the ICU doors interrupted us.

"Where is he?" a man shouted. "Where's Eric?"

Within seconds the man burst through the doors and hurried toward Eric's alcove. He almost shoved a nurse's aide out of the way to get next to Eric's bed. I could tell it was his father by the way he spoke. He asked the doctor a lot of questions, one right after the other, but never waited for an answer. Finally one of the doctors took him down the hallway and talked with him. I could see his shoulders slump and his eyes look down as the doctor spoke. I could tell that the doctor had made him feel better. They walked back in my direction and then turned into the alcove where Eric was. His dad sat down on a stool.

He whispered into Eric's ears, "It's okay, buddy." I could barely make out his words. "You're going to be okay. I'm here." He spoke continually, lightly stroking Eric's arm and ignoring the doctors and nurses as they worked around him. Only the beeping of a heart monitor could be heard, that and the soft voice of Eric's dad.

I suddenly felt very much out of place. I turned and wheeled out of the ICU area and headed back to my room. I felt guilty. I felt awful. What had I done? I had abandoned Eric. The door must have locked shut behind him, and he must have tried to get back in. I wasn't there to hear him knocking for help. I tried to tell myself there must have been some other reason why he got caught on the roof, but I couldn't think of any. There was only one answer: I had abandoned him.

Hours later I was in bed, staring out into the dark.

The wind howled outside, and a tree branch scraped against the window. I shuddered every time I thought of what it must have been like for Eric to be outside in the cold and dark. Every time the thought struck me, I gasped, like I was calling out to God—like I was calling out to God for Eric.

I prayed that night for the first time in a long time. It was as if Jesus were in the room, sitting on the chair across from me. I knew I wanted Eric to live, not just because I was feeling guilty about leaving him out in the cold, but because I really missed him. And because I believed he *should* live. I remembered his smile when I was feeling my worst. I remembered his kind eyes. I remembered his honesty. I remembered how he wasn't afraid to show everyone who he was—a weird-looking kid who was glad he was alive. I couldn't imagine someone like Eric not being able to live. I prayed that he would live. I prayed a lot.

❊ ❊ ❊

I went back to ICU early the next morning, not waiting for my mom or dad to visit me in my room first. The staff on the ICU floor were all different, except for one doctor that I remembered from the night before. I approached him and got up the courage to ask, "How's Eric?"

He looked at me over the edge of his glasses as he wrote on a chart. "Are you a relative?"

"Ah, no. I'm Darcy. I was here last night. I . . . the nurse said I could be here."

"Well, Eric is still very, very sick. We don't know what his body will do yet, but it doesn't look good. He's a fighter, but this battle he's fighting is bigger than any he's faced before."

I looked in the direction of Eric's room.

"Do you want to go down there?" the doctor asked.

I nodded.

"I'll ask Mr. Jenkins if you can come in." The doctor left and then returned shortly. "Go ahead. He wants to meet you."

I hesitated. I didn't think Eric's dad would know who I was. I didn't move. The doctor put his hand on my shoulder. "Go ahead. It's okay. He really wants to meet you," he said.

That's what I'm afraid of, I thought. But I couldn't explain it to the doctor. I just went ahead and hoped for the best. I slowly wheeled my way around a couple of medicine carts until I reached Eric's alcove. I waited a moment and then went in, up to the end of the bed. Eric's father was sitting in a small chair and had his back to me. He was leaning over Eric's face. He heard my wheels squeak. He turned.

"So you're Darcy," he said.

I nodded in a shy kind of way.

"Eric's talked about you."

"Oh?"

"Yes. Every night he'd come home from this hospital and tell me about meeting you and what you've been going through."

I must have looked confused because he said, " I hope you don't mind that he told me. He just asked me for ideas about how he could help you."

"No, I don't mind. I guess I was a 'hard case' to solve."

"Maybe. But for now the hard case is Eric," he said as he turned toward his son. "Doctors don't think—" He halted and then continued, "They don't think he'll make it through the day."

I breathed in sharply. I was stunned. I hadn't prepared myself for Eric to be this bad. *But I had prayed! God, why won't You heal him now?* I had never been in a situation like this before, and I didn't know what to say—or if I should say anything. My emotions took over, and I blurted, "It doesn't make sense." Mr. Jenkins turned to me with a serious look on his face. I paused, shook my head, and added, "Why would this happen?"

He leaned back in the chair. There was a long stretch of silence, and then Mr. Jenkins said softly, "Good question. I've thought about that a lot." There was more silence, and it gave the whole scene a heavy sense of importance. Mr. Jenkins took a deep breath and then said, "But I think I've found the answer, Darcy. And I think Eric helped me to find it. In fact, I *know* he helped me find it. Can I tell you what I learned?"

I nodded. I really wanted to know.

"It's not a nice story, and I'm not proud of what happened. You see, the fire that burned Eric so badly? Well, I started it." He stopped, closed his eyes, and held Eric's hand. He was choked up, unable to speak.

For some weird reason, I didn't feel nervous about being with this adult who was on the verge of tears. I desperately wanted to comfort him. "You mean that it was some mistake that you made that caused it?" I asked.

He turned back toward me and shook his head. It was a long while before he spoke. "No. I *started* it. On purpose. I was drunk."

Those last words almost made me gasp.

Mr. Jenkins took another deep breath and continued, "I was angry that night about something I can't even remember. I think it had something to do with Eric and his chores. But it was more than that. I was just angry at everyone and everything. I went crazy and took a stick out of the fireplace that had a small flame on it. I was swinging it and threatening Eric for not doing what he was supposed to do. Eric just stared at me. That made me all the more angry. I started yelling at him and then . . . I don't know what happened next. I thought I threw the stick back in the fire, but all I remember is the sight of the curtains of our house going up in flames. They seemed to just explode, like they had gasoline on them or something. I tried to get hold of myself, but that awful alcohol . . ."

Mr. Jenkins shook his head in disgust. "I panicked when I saw the fire spread. I got scared and ran out of the house, leaving my family inside. I didn't call the fire department. They told me later that Eric did that. His mom had panicked. And his younger brother and sister were just little ones. They found them huddled with their mom in the corner of the bedroom. Eric, they said, had been trying to drag them out, but my wife wouldn't let him. Finally Eric ran through the house trying to find a place to escape. A fireman found him in time before the smoke got to him.

"The boy didn't cry, the firemen told me later, even though he was burned all over. He was in shock. It wasn't until he got to the hospital that the pain began. They gave him painkillers, but it didn't help. Every day seemed to get worse. They had to peel skin from one part of his body to put on parts that were badly burned. Grafting, they called it. I called it torture. His screams were too much to bear. I left after the second day and—"

Mr. Jenkins suddenly got this pained look on his face—disgust at himself. "Can you believe I didn't come back to the hospital? I couldn't watch Eric go through that pain. Not after what I'd done to him. I know I should have stayed, even if he hated me. He needed me. He had no mother to comfort him either."

Mr. Jenkins broke down, softly sobbing for several minutes. His shoulders shook. After a few minutes, he reached across the bed table for a Kleenex to wipe his eyes and nose.

I just stared in the direction of the heart monitor at the side of Eric's headboard. I couldn't say anything. I was amazed at Eric—all he had gone through. My accident seemed like nothing compared to what he had to experience. I don't think I could have done what he did.

But then I remembered that it was Mr. Jenkins who had started this story in order to tell me something important, to tell me what Eric had taught him. I turned my eyes from the heart monitor and moved a little closer to Eric's dad. I still wanted to know what this all meant.

"Mr. Jenkins," I said after a minute, "you said you knew why. Can you tell me?"

He nodded and began talking again, this time in a softer voice. "Darcy, the amazing thing about Eric is not that he survived. It's not that he tried to save his family while I did nothing. It's not that he acts as if there's nothing wrong with his looks. And it's not that he comes back here to help kids feel good about themselves. It's not any of those things. What's amazing about Eric is that he forgave me."

He turned and looked me directly in the eyes. "He forgave me. He said to me one day when I came back to visit him in the hospital, 'Dad, it's okay. I forgive you.' Then he gave me this."

Mr. Jenkins reached into his pocket and held out a stone. It was dark, reddish, and smooth. "He called it a Givestone."

"A what?"

"Givestone. Short for 'I-forgive-you stone,' he told

me. He gave it to me after he came out of the hospital the last time. He made up the word and told me that he wanted me to have it as a reminder that he forgave me. And he wanted me to know that God's forgiven me, too. My son said that I should carry it with me all the time to remind myself that I'm forgiven, that Jesus forgave me when I told Him how sorry I was." At this point Mr. Jenkins clutched the stone and held his hand up. He managed a smile—a proud smile—and said, "Some kid, huh?"

"Yeah," I said. It was hard to take it all in, almost hard to believe. But not hard to believe either. Eric was like that. Just an incredible, unusual kid. "But still, Mr. Jenkins, why does this happen? And why doesn't Eric get better?"

"Eric might still get better, Darcy. Oh, I want him so much to get better," he said sadly as he turned to look at his boy in the bed. Then he sighed and continued, "But if he doesn't . . . if he doesn't get better, what does matter is that God's got something a whole lot more important than our bodies in mind. He'll let really hard things happen to get at what's most important— our hearts. In Eric's case it was *my* heart God was after. He used Eric to get through to my angry, drunken heart. And he used Eric's forgiveness to heal it."

"But that doesn't seem fair. Why does Eric have to go through all the hard stuff instead of—"

"Instead of me?" he interrupted. "I don't have all the answers yet. But I do know this, whenever someone talks about how unfair it was for Jesus to die on the cross, I understand." He paused. "I can understand how unfair things can be."

The sound of Eric's heart monitor pulsed slowly, loudly. I wondered about the kind of heart that was underneath the ugly skin and distorted face. Eric was different from me. Very different. He had found something I didn't have. And he had changed someone's life, someone as awful as his father.

And he was changing me, too.

"Mr. Jenkins," I said slowly, "I have to tell you something. I . . ." I couldn't look at his face, and so I turned and faced Eric. "It's my fault. It's my fault that Eric's sick. I left him outside yesterday. We were on the roof. . . . He was, not me. I couldn't get up the stairs. I was supposed to wait for him to come back with a ramp. But I got scared. I left him behind. He probably knocked hard to get back in, but I wasn't there. I had gone and left him. I—I'm . . ." All of my fears and guilt let go in a flood of tears. I grabbed a corner of Eric's bed sheet and pressed it against my cheek. Slowly I leaned over against his bed and buried my face in his blanket to muffle my tears.

It wasn't very long before Mr. Jenkins placed his large hands on my shoulders and stroked my hair. He was silent as he did so, but I heard him cry a little, too. It made my sadness feel all the worse. I sat up and wiped my hand across my eyes. We just sat there quietly, waiting for Eric to do something, say something . . . anything. The only sounds were the breathing machine and the heart monitor beeping.

I wondered if I would ever be happy again.

Six

It was much later when Mr. Jenkins walked me back down to my room and said good-bye. I got myself ready for bed, slid in off my wheelchair, and pulled the covers up over my mouth. The room was dark with only the light from the nurse's station coming through the doorway. I turned my head toward the empty chair where I had imagined Jesus sitting the night before. I decided to try to pray.

I had talked to Him so easily before. But tonight was different. I could barely put words together in my mind, let alone say them out loud. Finally, feeling desperate, I simply said what was on my mind: "God, I don't have what Eric has. I could never do what he did. I could never forgive like that. Please help me."

As I lay staring at the empty chair, memories of Sunday school and the things my teachers taught me came to mind. It was a kids' song I remembered first. "Jesus loves me, this I know . . ." Then for some reason I remembered a real old hymn that they sang in our church, one that I hadn't really liked all that much. "Would you be free from your burden of sin? There's power in the blood, power in the blood. . ." I didn't know why it struck me, but I suddenly knew why the truth in this hymn was important. I did want to be free from this burden I felt.

Then the Bible memory work that I had done as a little kid in Bible Day Camp popped into my head. "If we confess our sins, he is faithful and just to forgive us our sins and to cleanse us from all unrighteousness." I knew I believed that and hoped that God would forgive me. I prayed believing that way.

But still something was missing.

* * *

"Wake up, Darcy, honey!" the Saturday nurse said, standing next to my bed along with my mom. The storms of the last few days had blown away, and the sun was shining brightly outside my window. "You sure is asleepin' late this mornin', child! What'd you do all last night? Watch cartoons?"

I rubbed my eyes and shook my head no. *It's too hard to explain*, I thought. The nurse didn't wait for an explanation.

My mom spoke instead. "Well, I've got great news, Darcy. The doctor says you can go home today. The pressure sore is something we can handle at home now. You won't miss Thanksgiving!"

I was still sleepy, and so the idea of going home didn't sink in. "How's Eric?" I asked.

"Eric? You mean the boy with the burns?" my mom asked.

"Yeah, he's up in ICU. Can I go see him, Mom, before we go home?" I propped myself up in bed and reached for my wheelchair. "I gotta see how he is."

"Whoa there, child, you ain't going nowhere till you do what I needs you to do. Last minute stuff before you check outta this hotel!" She took the electronic thermometer and stuck it in my ear. Within seconds it beeped and let her know I had no fever. "Cool, child. You's cool. Now give me your arm and let me hear how that blood's pumpin." She did the blood pressure check and then checked my pulse. Everything was fine.

"Now can I go?" I asked the nurse.

"Now you can go," she answered.

Up until now, I had been in hospital pajamas and robes. But today it was back to my old jeans and sweater sets. It took longer than I had expected to get dressed, but I made it. It had been three weeks since doing that kind of thing, and I was tired by the time I zipped up my pants. My mom helped me sit up and get into the wheelchair. "You look a little pale," she said. "Hard work?"

I nodded, got myself comfortable in the chair, and as Mom helped me button my sweater, said halfway under my breath, "Mind if I go say good-bye to a friend?" Before I gave her much time to think about it, I headed for the door. I left the room, figuring that she had stuff to do, like cleaning out my room closet and side tables. It wasn't until I reached the elevator that I realized I was alone. I was glad for it. I wanted to see Eric alone. Somehow, without saying a word, he had taught me a lot. I wanted to tell him what I had learned from him. From Jesus.

I got off the elevator and almost thought it was the wrong floor. The doors of ICU were propped open, and everything seemed different. The hustle of the previous two days was now gone. One nurse sat at the desk eating a doughnut, and another talked on the phone.

A doctor stood quietly outside a patient's alcove and read a chart. The hallway was clear of portable machines and IV poles. A janitor mopped the floor. I had to move closer to Eric's area to be sure I was in the right place.

"Looking for someone?" the nurse with the doughnut asked.

"Yeah, Eric."

Her eyes squinted a little. She looked at the chart, then toward Eric's alcove. She looked in the direction of the doctor. "Doctor Harding, could you come here a minute?" she said.

He approached me and looked to the nurse for an explanation. "She wants to see Eric," she said.

By this time I already knew it was bad news. The doctor kneeled down by the side of my wheelchair and tucked his clipboard under his arm. People had been telling me bad news for most of my life like this. The doctor took a deep breath, but I decided to speak first.

"He died, didn't he?" I asked directly.

The doctor nodded. "Last night. Real peaceful."

"Was his dad here?"

"Yes. He's still here, in fact. Downstairs, I think. Did you want to see him?"

I nodded. He picked up the phone and called some

office. At this point my feelings began to catch up with me, and I started to cry. The nurse came next to me and held me. "Was he a friend?" she asked.

I couldn't answer. The nurse felt sympathy for me and took hold of my wheelchair. I didn't mind. She pushed me toward the elevator and took me downstairs to the small chapel next to the main lobby of the hospital. She wheeled me through the door. It was a cozy, small place, and light streamed in through a colored window. Just as the nurse was leaving, Mr. Jenkins came in. He had just finished taking care of Eric's things. "I'm glad I got to see you, Darcy," he said as he closed the door of the chapel. "I wanted to tell you something. And I wanted to leave you this." He pulled out a stone, the Givestone he had shown me the day before.

"Why?" I asked.

"I've been holding on to this stone a long time, Darcy. It's been a good reminder for me. But I don't need it anymore. I'll never forget Eric. And I'll never forget that he forgave me."

He took my hand, placed the stone in the center, and closed my fingers around it. "You need to keep this now. 'Cause you need to remember."

"Remember what?"

"That Eric forgave you . . . and I forgive you, too."

I hugged Mr. Jenkins and held on for a long time. I said I was sorry a dozen times, and he said that I didn't need to worry about saying I was sorry. I clutched the Givestone and kept thanking him. He said it was okay. I cried again.

The chapel was quiet except for me sniffling. Finally, Mr. Jenkins grabbed both my hands and squeezed them together and said, "Darcy, it's time for me to go." He stood up and patted my shoulder. "And I hear you're goin' home today. That's good. Neither one of us has a reason to stay here now," he said. Then slowly he turned and left.

I stayed behind in the chapel for a little while longer, holding the Givestone tightly in my hand.

* * *

My mom and I left the hospital an hour later, filling out a bunch of forms and then saying good-bye to as many nurses and aides as I knew from the weekend shift. Unlike the first time I left Willowbrook Rehab four years ago, this exit was quiet and without lots of cheering by the staff. We just hugged them and thanked them for their help. They all wished me the best and gave advice on how to stay out of pressure-sore trouble next time.

The ride home was just as quiet. I sat in the front seat, looking at the scenery to see if things had changed. Things had. Everyone seemed to be getting ready for Christmas even before Thanksgiving. Wreaths and garlands were hung. I could see the green wire of Christmas lights hung from windows and eaves. Plastic Santas and manger scenes dotted the lawns of homes here and there. They looked tacky in the daylight, and I thought they were up way too soon before Christmas. I loved Christmas and wished in many ways that people would put me in charge of Christmas altogether so that I could decide who decorated what and where, what music was played and how often, and even the kind of Christmas trees people should buy—Douglas fir, of course. Or Norwegian spruce. And only white light bulbs. No blinking ones either.

I would have been even more excited about Christmas, but something else occupied my mind. It was Eric. I pictured his face, even though it was hard to look at. I remembered his eyes, his lighthearted voice, his odd smile. I remembered our times together—the times he talked about the smallest details in life, the times he tried to cheer me up, even the times we fought. I realized how much of a friend he was and that I had not treated him well. *But he forgave me!*

I suddenly remembered the Givestone. I had not let go of it since Mr. Jenkins gave it to me in the chapel earlier in the day. I opened my hand to take a closer look. It was egg-shaped but flat. It was more of a burgundy color than reddish brown, and it was covered with tan specks. Its surface was soft to the touch but not smooth. Only when a tear dropped from my eye onto the stone did I notice how bright its color truly was. It looked warm. I held it to my cheek and stared out the window.

I rode that way for quite a while, lost in my thoughts of Eric and what I had learned while in the hospital, when suddenly Mom screamed, and I felt myself being thrown forward. The car screeched to a halt almost sideways. Mom had thrown her arm in front of me, but the seat belt had also held me tight. I looked at her and then at the scene in front of me. There, in the middle of the road, was a young boy about my age with a football in his hand. He stood about three feet from our car, staring wide-eyed at us.

My mom breathed out a "whew" and rolled down the window. "Watch what you're doing!" she said as we drove by slowly. The boy felt embarrassed but relieved to be safe. He ran back to the yard where other boys were standing.

"He ran out after the ball," my mom said as she began driving again. "I didn't see him until he was just about in front of us. Scared me to death." Her breath was short, her face flustered. She wasn't angry, just upset.

"Kind of like my accident, huh?" I said.

She nodded. She didn't say anything, but I could tell she was thinking about it. I did, too. Being on this side of the accident gave me a different feeling about it. It happened so quickly. I wondered what it was like for the driver of the car that hit me. I had come out of nowhere, too. What did he think about in that flash of a second before hitting me? Was he mad at me? Was he frightened?

The memory of my accident came rushing back to me, except this time it wasn't so much the sensations of the accident. It was more the feelings I had had. I remembered especially when I lay on the street and watched the tires of the sports car take off. I remembered the hot surge of anger at that driver. My cries were filled not only with pain but with anger. I remembered my words now. "Stupid!" I had yelled over and over again. "Stupid! Stupid!" I could feel the anger build even now as I remembered the scene. It was as if I were right there, experiencing it all over again. I shook my head to stop the feelings.

I looked over at my mom, who had calmed down by now and was driving normally. Then I looked down, opened up my hands, and stared at the Givestone in my palm. It was then I knew the one thing that held me back from being happy, from being like Eric.

I had never forgiven the person who hit me. I had been mad all of these years and hadn't realized it. Though I didn't wake up each morning with feelings of anger toward the driver, I had grown up thinking that someone had hurt me. I was paralyzed because of someone else. I was in a wheelchair because of someone else. I was unable to enjoy lots of things in my life because of someone else.

I clutched my Givestone tightly. I knew what I had to do, what I wanted to do. I wanted to forgive that driver. I wanted to let go of every bad feeling I had. I wanted to be happy. And not only would I forgive him in my mind, I would also say so out loud to him. I would track him down, no matter how long it took, and say that it was okay and that I forgave him.

Coming to the decision to forgive had an incredible effect on me. I felt light, as if someone really did lift my burden. I stared out the window at the row of trees on our street as we went by and whispered softly to myself just to be sure it was real, "I forgive you, whoever you are. Wherever you are. It's okay."

My mom looked at me but did not say anything. She pulled into the driveway and parked just outside the garage. "Are you ready, Darcy?" she asked.

"Oh, yeah. I'm ready. You bet I'm ready."

I was indeed ready. And I would find the person who hit me and forgive him. No matter what it took to find him, I would wheel up to him someday and let him know that I didn't blame him anymore.

Seven

"Pass the potatoes, please."

"Are there oysters in this stuffing, Dad?"

"Who's got the other turkey leg?"

"Oysters? Not this year. I ran out. Just clams."

"Yuuk!"

"Just kidding. But you wait—some year I will put oysters in the stuffing, and you're going to find out how good it is."

The joy of Thanksgiving dinner lasted long into the evening. We had awakened to the sound of Mom in the kitchen rattling pots and pans. By mid-morning we were all poking around in the kitchen to sample a little bit of stuffing or lick the bowl of any leftover pumpkin filling. By noon the whole house smelled great from roasted turkey fresh out of the oven. By one o'clock we had started eating and just kept eating and talking for the rest of the afternoon. Mostly we talked. There was a lot of catching up to do, partly because I had been gone for three weeks. For me, though, it seemed as if I was catching up on five years of being apart from the family.

Monica said it best during pumpkin pie. "You know, Darcy, you used to be '*numero uno* jerk-o' most of the time. It was always about you and your chair or your therapy or your 'I wish I could do that' pouty face. This new you is definitely the way to go. Right, Mom?"

"What do you mean by 'new you'?" my mom asked.

"I don't know." Monica shrugged and licked her dessert plate with her finger. "It's just that when Darcy first came in the door, she was asking questions about how we were doing. And she didn't whine."

"Yeah. And she didn't even yell at me when I showed her how I busted her CD player!" Josh added.

I was glad they had noticed. I sat quietly, thankful that God was beginning to make an honest-to-goodness change in me.

My mom finally answered Monica's question.

"Well, Darcy did have her moments. Maybe we thought too much about what Darcy was suffering rather than what she should have been learning. What do you think, dear?" My mom turned to my dad.

"Whatever you say, dear. Now cut me another piece of that pie."

"George!"

"Just kidding," Dad joked. "You are different, Darcy. Most of the time I like to look for changes in people over a long period of time, but there's definitely something different about you deep down inside. Hold on to that, you hear?"

"I will, Dad," I said.

A pause in our conversation arrived. I took the chance to announce what I had thought about on the car ride home. "Uh, I have an idea about how to hold on to this, Dad."

"Oh? What is it?"

"Well, I've been thinking about Eric and something I learned from him and from his father. It's about forgiveness. You see, I've been mad at a lot of people for no good reason. Like Monica said, I've been a real jerk. I've learned that I need to forgive people and that when I do that, I'm doing something Jesus did. And it's something Jesus commanded me to do."

Monica rolled her eyes a bit. "And the point is . . ."

"I'm getting to that." I resisted the temptation to make some nasty comment. Monica was a great sister but not so strong in the patience category. "You know the guy that hit me? The guy with the red Corvette? I'd like to forgive him."

"That's nice," my dad said, with a piece of pie almost to his mouth. "But you already told us how you've forgiven people. Why is forgiving the driver who hit you some new idea?"

"Uh, you don't understand. I need to forgive him in person, Dad. You know, face to face."

My mom's fork stopped in midair. My dad's face went blank for a moment. He looked over at my mom and then at me. Everyone else stopped eating their desserts, too, as though I had just dropped a bomb in the middle of the table.

Dad was the first to speak. "I'm not sure that would be a good idea, Darcy."

"But, Dad!" I interrupted. "I have to! You don't understand!"

As soon as those words escaped my mouth, I knew I had spoken them too fast and too harshly. And a little too loudly. Dad didn't like it when we kids did that, even if we were right about something. I deserved what came next.

"Contrary to what you think, I do understand, Darcy. But first you're not going to do anything with that tone of voice. You'll sit quietly in your room after dinner for an hour. And as for your idea, there are reasons why I don't think it's a good idea for you to meet this man—reasons your mother and I don't want to share right now."

My "but" was forming on my lips when Josh changed the subject, mumbling, "Why do people put oysters in turkey stuffing anyway?"

✱ ✱ ✱

I lay on my bed facing the ceiling during the one-hour "time out." I could hear the TV on down the hall and Josh watching a Charlie Brown Thanksgiving special. I could hear the cold November wind blowing outside my window, and that made the comforter on my bed feel all the more warm. It was a great place to think. Besides, I knew I deserved being sent to my room. And that was okay, because the quiet time helped me to devise a plan—a plan to find out who the driver was.

It seemed a little sneaky at first, but I thought about what my dad had said. First, he didn't say that I shouldn't find out his name. And, second, he said that he didn't think it was a good idea. That wasn't a direct order, in my way of thinking. It was just an opinion.

And so I felt the freedom to explore how I might find this mysterious person. I wanted the man to know the same happiness I had found. I pictured our meeting. He'd see me and feel awkward, maybe start to cry. I'd say it was okay and that God had a reason for all of this. We'd talk for a while. And then maybe he'd come to our house. Maybe he had a family, and so both our families could get together and be friends. For life. The more I thought of it, the grander the scenes became in my mind.

I called my friends Chip, Mandy, and April when my hour was up. They were all classmates of mine. Chip was my best guy friend. He and I had grown up just three houses down from each other. We shared secrets, pulled pranks, and cheered each other up. He was the steady one of the four of us, always thinking. Whenever we wanted to know whether or not something was good to do or not, we looked to Chip. Of course, he annoyed us once in a while by being so responsible. But he kept us out of trouble more often than not. At least when we listened.

Mandy was a good listener and always tried to look on the good side of things. She wouldn't get overly excited about things or get too mad either.

April, on the other hand, was Miss Melodramatic. Everything was a big deal. But she was a great encourager, and she wasn't afraid of anything.

I called Chip first.

"Chip? This is Darcy. Listen . . . huh? Yeah, I'm fine. But listen, we have to get together tomorrow. You call Mandy and April, and we'll meet at your house, okay? . . . No, not here. I'll tell you why later."

***

The next morning was Friday after Thanksgiving. That meant a breakfast of turkey leftovers, which was fine with me. I was anxious to meet my friends over at Chip's house, and so I wasted no time in scarfing down breakfast, straightening my room, bundling up, and heading out the door. When I arrived, Mandy and April were already there. I hugged the girls and almost hugged Chip, I was so happy to see everyone. We talked a little about my hospital stay and the healed pressure sore, and then we moved into Chip's kitchen. Everybody pulled up chairs, and we got down to business.

"Okay, Darcy, cough it up. What sneaky plan are you up to this time?" April demanded.

"It's not sneaky. And it's not a plan, really. At least not yet. First, let me tell you guys something. I changed while I was in the hospital."

"Oh, so you got one of those nose jobs? I thought you looked different," Mandy teased.

"No, get serious, guys. I met a boy named Eric—"

"Ah! I should have known it. Of course it's a boy. Darcy's in love! Sorry, Chipster. You'll have to find some other 'physically challenged' person to marry!" April smirked.

"April! Cut it out. Let Darcy tell her story," Chip growled.

"Thank you, Chip. And besides, April, Eric died."

April was stunned. "Oh, I'm so sorry," she said sincerely.

"It's okay, April. Not your stupid remarks but him dying, I mean. Not that dying is a good thing, but . . . oh, it's too hard to explain. I'll miss him, but the important thing is what he taught me." I told them what I had learned from Eric. They all listened quietly, nodding in agreement when I talked about how angry I usually was about things and how I thought about myself. I realized just how good these friends were. They had put up with my attitude and didn't walk away from me through all these years.

"So now what you're telling us is that Darcy's perfect, right? So why are we here?"

"No, I'm not perfect. And you're here because I need your help. Do you remember the guy who drove the car that hit me?"

"Not really," Mandy replied. "It's not like we met him afterwards at a barbecue or something."

"You know what I mean. You remember that there was a guy, right? And that he drove a red Corvette convertible."

"Yeah. So?" Chip questioned.

"So . . . I want to meet him." I quickly scanned the eyes of my friends.

They looked at each other weird-like and then at me. "Why do you want to do that?" Mandy asked.

"Why doesn't anyone get it?" I said, exasperated. "I want him to know that I forgive him—that's why!" I wheeled away from the kitchen table where we were all sitting and moved into the family room. I sat looking out the window into the backyard. The others followed me a short while later.

"Darcy," Chip said as they sat down on the floor in front of me, "it's not that we think you're crazy or anything. It's just that, well, don't you think that he wouldn't have driven away from the accident when he first hit you if he felt bad? And if he wanted to be forgiven, he would have come to see you by now to say he's sorry."

"But that's the whole point about forgiving, Chip. We're supposed to forgive someone whether or not they say they're sorry. And, besides, maybe he's really sorry, but he's too afraid. Maybe he thinks we'll sue him or something. Have you ever thought of that? No, I really believe I'm supposed to go to him and tell him how I feel."

My friends exchanged glances with each other and then looked at me. "Darcy," Chip spoke for all of them, "we'll help you with whatever you need. Maybe you know something we don't know. We'll trust you on this one."

"Great, guys! Oh, this is going to be so awesome. I can't wait."

"So, what do we do first?" Mandy got us started.

"I've been thinking about that. My idea was to find out first who it was that hit me."

"Do your folks know?" Mandy asked. "Did you ask them?"

"Well, kind of. I'm not sure if they know who it is or not. My dad wasn't so keen on the idea. But . . ." I raised my hand as I saw Chip begin to object. "He only said he didn't think it was a good idea. He didn't tell me not to. So this mission isn't against the law."

"Okay, so your mom and dad may or may not know. And this person may or may not even live around here. Or even still be alive, which is a very real possibility given the way he drives and—"

"I hear you, April," I interrupted. "But let's assume he is alive and that he's still around. Where do we start?"

"Police, I say," suggested Mandy.

"Yeah, of course. They'd have info if they ever did find out who the driver was. Let's try it." Chip went to get his phone. I loved Chip for how he did things. Once an idea was decided upon, he'd just do things without any fear. "Hello," he said when he heard someone on the line. "Can I speak to someone who keeps track of information about accidents?"

Chip was put on hold for a few moments. "Yes, I'd like information about an accident that happened five years ago. My friend Darcy DeAngelis was hit by a car, and we're trying to find out who the driver was. Yes, DeAngelis. . . . Five years ago on Arbor Street. It was a red Corvette."

We waited as Chip listened.

"Oh, okay. . . . Yeah, I understand. . . . Well, she's twelve. . . . She's my friend. . . . Okay. Well, thanks anyway." Chip hung up the phone.

"Strike one," he said. "The police won't give us that information. You're supposed to get it from your parents. You're too young."

"Yep, that's strike one, all right," said April. "In fact, that sounds like the whole game right there, Darcy. Maybe you'll get on the *Oprah Winfrey Show* some other time." She laughed, not to make fun but to cheer me up.

"Thanks for the moral support, April," I said. "But it's not over yet."

We sat in silence for a while until Chip suddenly burst out, "I've got it!"

"What?" we all asked.

"He drove a red 'Vette,' right? And 'Vette' owners usually hang out with other 'Vette' owners! That's the answer."

"Darcy, tell your boyfriend there to speak English. We girls don't get it," April urged.

"It's simple. We find out if there are any Corvette clubs in the area. Then we try and track down any members who own a red one. All we'd have to do is describe the car to someone, and they'd probably give us some clues!"

"Great idea, Chip!" I said. Mandy nodded. April finally agreed. The hunt was on.

Eight

Chip's idea was brilliant. Sort of.

"So, where do we find a Corvette club?" I asked.

"Let's check the phone book," Mandy answered. Chip went to the kitchen and returned with one. He searched through the Yellow Pages for automobiles, then cars, then Corvettes, then clubs. Nothing.

"Okay, what's next?" Chip asked.

"How about the library?" I answered.

"Closed today," Mandy said.

"Maybe we could call a car dealer in town. He might know," Chip volunteered.

"Same as the library. Probably closed on the day after Thanksgiving," Mandy repeated.

"Guys! Get with it, will ya!" April scolded. "You'd think you people were living in the Stone Age. Let's surf, dudes!"

"You mean the Internet?" I asked.

"Duh. Give that girl a Twinkie. Of course, the Internet. C'mon, let's go to my house. I've got a Pentium with a great modem. We'll have Corvette clubs coming out the screen . . ."

April's voice trailed off as she ran out the door ahead of us. We followed her to her house about a quarter of a mile away. It was a lot nicer home than any of ours, with all the latest gadgets and cars. April had her own private room in addition to her bedroom. It was a combination playroom and study. Computer, stereo, TV, beanbags, and electronic games filled the room. We gathered around the monitor and watched as April logged onto the Net.

"Okay, what should we start with?" she queried.

"Let's go with Corvette club," Chip suggested.

April typed in the words and waited a few seconds.

"Great. Just 18,438 entries to look at. Any other brilliant ideas before we start looking through all of this?"

"Try Willowbrook Corvette Club just in case we get lucky," Mandy urged.

"Okay, but they'd have to be a pretty boring group

of people to come up with an unoriginal name like that," April said as she typed in Mandy's suggestion. We waited a few more seconds.

Suddenly April yelled, "I can't believe it! There's one site. And it's a perfect match!"

"So, c'mon. Go to the site," I said. "Let's see what it's got."

The web page had a picture of a Corvette, of course, and listings of car shows being held in our state. We went to the Directory section, hoping to find a name there, but all we saw were listings of other clubs in other areas. We went back to the home page.

"Maybe this one will have something," Chip said as he pointed to the spot marked Gallery. April clicked the mouse on the icon, and we all waited. When the downloading was complete, we found something we thought we could use.

"Look. These are pictures of the members of the club with their cars. This is it! This is what we're looking for!" Mandy jumped out of her chair and shook April's shoulders. "Great surfing, April! You did it!"

We watched the screen as car after car went by. It was amazing how many cars there were in just one club. We saw some that came close to what we thought the red car had looked like, but in each case we were disappointed. "Wrong year," someone would say. "Darcy's accident happened two years before that model came out." Or, "Nope, can't be that one. How about that one? It's red, and it could be the right year. But, look, it's not a convertible. We all remember it as a convertible, right?"

Finally, on the last picture of the Gallery, we found it. A group picture of about twenty-five people all standing around a "Vette." Each one of us started looking at the people's faces.

"Do you remember what he looked like?" Mandy asked.

I shrugged my shoulders, worried that I wouldn't remember.

I stared at each person's face carefully. I was on the man standing four places from the left when I caught a face out of the corner of my eye. The man was standing on the far right—a short man with dark, thinning hair.

"That's him!" I yelled. "That's him! I know it is!"

"Are you sure? It was five years ago," Chip said. "And it happened so fast. How can you be sure?"

"Because that's him! It's the same leather jacket. And the same glasses. I'm telling you, that's the man!"

We all stared and didn't say a word. It was weird, seeing the person who hit me. I tried to imagine from the picture what he sounded like. His smile seemed nice enough, but we all had this suspicion that he was a crook or something.

"Probably with the Mafia," April said.

"Or sells drugs," Mandy added.

"Or both," Chip said slowly. "This could be dangerous, guys. Finding out who did it is one thing. Actually trying to find him may not be a good idea."

I shook my head. "Look, this is not TV. This is real life in Willowbrook. The man's not a drug dealer or a Mafia crook!" I tried to sound convincing even though I knew I might be wrong. I didn't want to be wrong. I couldn't be wrong. This person was just an ordinary person that I wanted to meet.

"What do we do now?" Mandy asked. "Take this man's picture to the police station and ask them if they've ever seen him before?"

"Now that would be a switch—policemen being asked that question," April laughed.

"No, we don't need to ask the policemen," Chip said. "Take a look." He pointed to the bottom of the web page. An address and phone number were printed in large letters. "This is a little too easy, don't you think?"

It wasn't that easy. We called the phone number and spoke to a man. We asked him about the photo and if he knew who the man was. He told us it was actually an older photo from many years earlier. "You could ask Joe Timmons though," he told us. "He was the president of the club at the time. He runs the auto shop down by the bus station. Doubt that he's got a computer though. You'll have to take a copy of the picture down there and show him."

We thanked the man for his help and hung up.

"The bus station! That's clear on the other side of town. Now what?" April asked.

"How about your brother? Could he drive us over there?"

"Maybe. If he's not stuck in front of the TV watching football. I'll go check. Meanwhile you guys print out the picture. We'll need that for Joe Timmons." April left the room, and Chip did the printing. A clear full-color picture printed out within a minute.

April popped back into the room. "Ryan will be happy to drive us, provided we buy him a hamburger and fries on the way. I just *love* my brother," she said sarcastically. "He's so unselfish!"

✴ ✴ ✴

Thirty minutes later we found ourselves on a side of town I had never visited before. The sidewalks were more cracked, and the stores on the corners were a lot older. It was the kind of neighborhood where you'd expect to find a mechanic shop easily. And driving up to the address and looking around, we could see clearly that Joe Timmons was the kind of auto mechanic they had back when my dad first started driving. A dozen or so old cars were lined up outside. Judging from the rust on the cars, you knew those weren't there to be repaired. It looked like his own personal junkyard. Inside the garage everything appeared to be covered with brown and gray dust mixed with grease. The smell of cigarette smoke was heavy in the air. A few bare light bulbs hung from the ceiling and provided the only light in the place.

The only thing that wasn't old or dirty was what we saw in the center of the garage—a silver Corvette. I wasn't into cars, but even I had to admit that this one was great. Chip and Ryan stared open-mouthed at the car, almost drooling. April and Mandy managed only to say "cool" and "awesome" and walked around it several times.

"Touch that car and you're dog meat!" a voice called out from the darkness. Mandy and April jumped back. I hid behind Ryan. We all stood frozen, unable to speak.

"What do ya want?" a man's voice gruffly asked. "Come to drop off a car?"

"Uh—uh, no!" Ryan stuttered. "Just these kids. I mean . . . these kids had a question. I just drove them here. Honest."

"So ask!" the man ordered. As he did so, he emerged from the shadows. What I saw made me laugh—almost. Unlike the evil figure that should have matched the big, fearsome voice, Mr. Timmons was quite small, with a plain, clean-shaven face. His hair was light, almost blond. He smiled broadly. We all exhaled, and he heard it.

"Sorry—didn't mean to scare you. That dog meat thing was just a joke. My name is Timmons. Joe Timmons. What can I do for you kids?"

I rolled forward and presented the picture. "This," I said, "came from the web site for the Corvette club. The man on the phone said you might know the people in the picture."

Mr. Timmons took it from me. "Oh, yeah, the computer web site. Don't own a computer myself, as you might guess from this place. I'm a little old-fashioned, you might say. Can't even convince myself to buy a new 'Vette.' This one from the '60s does just fine for me. Anyway, who do you want to know about in this picture?"

I wheeled up beside him and pointed to the man on the right. "That one."

Mr. Timmons's eyes narrowed as he studied the picture. "What you want to know about him?"

"Well, his name for one thing."

"Why?"

"Uh, well . . ." I hesitated and began fishing for some explanation.

Chip stepped forward. "It's kind of personal, sir. But, you see, Darcy was in an accident. We think this man was there. She—we wanted to meet him and ask him some questions."

Mr. Timmons looked at Chip. "And who are you?"

"A friend of Darcy's," he answered, pointing at me. "We go to the same school."

Mr. Timmons looked at the picture a long time. "Well, that there is Frank Germain. Used to be in the club but quit a while back. Don't know why. Just came into the shop here one day and said he'd sold his 'Vette' and wasn't in the club anymore. Just like that. Haven't seen him since."

"Do you know if he still lives around here?" I asked.

"Couldn't tell you that. Like I said, he just quit and walked away. Odd though—that 'Vette' of his was a beaut. And worth a lot of money, too. It was a special edition, and if he had held off selling it till now, he could have had an easy twenty grand."

"Wow!" April said. "He sounds like an idiot to me."

"April!" Mandy scolded her.

"Well, it's true," April argued. "Anyway, you got the info you needed, Darcy, so let's go. We've got to get this gorilla brother of mine a hamburger before he charges us double."

We spent another few minutes admiring the Corvette before leaving. Mr. Timmons was happy to show off his prized possession. He showed us the engine. It was cleaner than my room! He came close to giving us a ride in it, but Ryan said we had to get going. We thanked the mechanic as we headed back to the car.

"Okay, now we have a name," I said as I slid from the wheelchair into Ryan's car. "What's next?"

"Back to the Internet, I'd say," Chip answered. "I think we're real close to meeting Mr. Germain."

* * *

We were close, but not close enough. Our search for Frank Germain came up with four addresses in town.

"Now what?" April asked. "Do we walk up to each one of these and say, 'Excuse us, but are you the Mafia drug dealer that drives red Corvettes over innocent little girls?'"

I made a face at her. April was usually over the edge in situations like this. It seemed, however, that we might have to do just that. We all stared at the four addresses.

"Guys, look," Chip said at last. "Let's think this through. First, look at these two addresses. This one says Golden Years Nursing Home. Now I know there are some old guys who like sports cars, but our guy isn't that old. And this other address—let's look at the map." Chip pulled up the map option that the Internet directory provided. "See, it's down here on First Avenue."

"So?"

"So the only thing on First Avenue are businesses. That means that if this is the guy we're looking for, it's just his office. It would mean that he's got a home address, too—one of these other two. And if I'm right, we now have to check out only two addresses instead of four." Chip looked at us as if we couldn't argue. We didn't.

"And there's more," Chip added. "Look at this one.

It's got two E-mail addresses. My hunch is that this one has his own web page. Let's check it out."

We typed in what we thought would be the address for the web page. Sure enough, a home page popped up on the screen. Frank Germain was typed in a Gothic font and spun in circles at the top of the screen. A picture of a boy about thirteen years old stared back at us.

"Doesn't look like Mafia to me," April observed. "So the other guy—"

"Must be *our* Frank Germain!" Mandy jumped up from her seat. "Oh, Darcy, isn't this exciting?"

"I guess," I answered. "Excited isn't the word now though. More like 'nervous.' I mean, now I have a man's name, face, and address. At least we think this is the man's address. If it is, then I actually can meet him. It's a little scary, guys."

The others were silent for a moment. Chip and Mandy nodded their heads. April whispered, "Whoa."

I breathed in deeply and sighed. This was not going to be as easy as I had thought.

Nine

I sat in my wheelchair at the end of the third pew on Sunday morning. Christmas lights were hung on two fake trees on the platforms. A big wreath hung behind the choir, which was singing "O Come, O Come, Emmanuel." One candle burned next to the open Bible on the table just in front of the podium.

It was getting close to Christmas, and the church was preparing.

I sat next to my family. It was one of the few times that we were all together at one time at church. It felt good sitting there, up close to the front. Dad sat next to me in the pew. He leaned over and said, "I'm starting to get into the Christmas spirit."

Dad loved Christmas. Ever since I could remember, he'd treat Christmas like he was still a kid and wanted each one to be the best ever. We always had to have a live tree. Christmas music was on all the time. And there were always Christmas rules about what you could or couldn't do. You couldn't eat fruitcake before December 20. You couldn't open any presents before Christmas day, even if a friend gave you one at school. You *had* to bring it home and put it under the tree. Dad loved Christmas.

The worship service was beautiful, and for the first time in a long time I listened closely. Even the boring parts weren't boring. I remembered everything the pastor said, not just his jokes. He talked about how people accept or reject God's gift of Jesus in the same way we receive gifts at Christmas. Some know they need Jesus and are excited when they first receive Him as Savior. They're thankful and can't wait to tell others. Other people, when they hear the good news about Jesus, either don't believe that eternal life is a gift, or they think it has to be earned, so they reject Jesus. They reject God's gift.

"Can you imagine what it's like for God to offer this free gift only to have so many people reject it?" the pastor asked. "It would make me want to give up on

Christmas altogether. I'm surprised God isn't a giant Scrooge after all these years of being rejected by so many people!"

I pictured God on Christmas morning, eagerly waiting for people to accept His gift. And then having each one shake the box, look at the wrapping, open it up, and then turn to God, and throw it back at Him. Or throw it in the wastebasket and go and get a different gift. *Sad*, I thought.

❊ ❊ ❊

As much as I enjoyed church, I was just as eager to get home. This would be the day that I would find Frank Germain. Saturday hadn't worked out because we all went shopping. And I didn't feel like asking Mom to take a detour for me to find this man. Actually, the truth is, I didn't think she'd approve.

Sunday lunch went by quickly, and I gladly chipped in to help Mom with the dishes. I wiped my hands on the towel and then excused myself to my room. I took out the map we had printed off the Internet. I had checked our town's bus routes and was relieved to see that one of the few routes with handicapped-accessible buses was on a street near Mr. Germain's house.

After I had all my stuff in order, I called Chip and asked if he could come with me. "At least as far as the street he lives on," I said. Chip agreed and said he'd meet me outside his house at 2:30. I left shortly before, telling my folks I'd be gone for about an hour on a walk with Chip.

Chip and I reviewed the map and headed off to the corner two blocks down where we could catch the bus. We timed it perfectly and got on board, heading in the direction of Frank Germain's house. The right Frank Germain, we hoped.

After a short ride, we got off and checked our map. The day was gray, but at least not raining as it had the day before. The air was warmer, too, and best of all, the wind was behind us. It pushed us on as we passed one block after another in record time. We stood at the corner of Foxwell Street and Binder Avenue before we knew it.

"Well, here it is," I said.

"Yeah. Do you want me come with you?"

"Ah . . . no. I think I'll do this myself. Just wait here, okay?"

"Sure thing."

I wheeled away from Chip and then turned around. "Chip?"

"Yeah?"

"Thanks. For being a good friend. You'll always be around, won't you." I said it more as a statement than as a question.

He answered as I knew he would. "Always. No matter where you go." He smiled and saluted with two fingers.

I turned back toward my destination—814 Foxwell Street. The houses on the street were built close to each other. They looked mostly the same except for the color of the paint. Cars were parked bumper to bumper on both sides of the street. The sidewalk was rough and cracked in many places. It was an older neighborhood. A bunch of kids played ball in the middle of the street. I wondered if one of them was Frank Germain's kid. Would he let his son play in the street knowing what could happen?

Thinking of Mr. Germain brought to mind my meeting with him. My stomach felt a big rush of heat go through it as fear set in. I had imagined the scene so many times in my mind that I felt as if I were rehearsing for a big play. *One last time.* I asked myself, *What are you going to do?*

I answered, *I'm going up to the door, ring the bell, and then wait. If a man comes to the door, I'll say, "Hi. I'm Darcy DeAngelis. I don't know if you remember me, but you hit me with your car five years ago." He'll be quiet for a few seconds, and then he's going to open the door and come out. He'll sit down on the edge of the concrete landing and cry. Or maybe just stare at me. Before I can say anything, he'll—*

The sound of a boy crying woke me out of my day-dream. The boy was standing on his front lawn, pointing at a Wiffle ball that was stuck in a tall bush. I looked to see if I could help and then realized that the boy was standing on the lawn of 814 Foxwell Street. This was it!

I slowed down my pace, trying to figure out what to do. Just then the front door opened. A man came out and headed toward the little boy. I breathed in sharply. It was him! Five years had not changed him much at all except for his hair. There was less of it now, but otherwise he was the same. My heart started to beat strongly. I felt my throat begin to tighten.

Mr. Germain noticed me as he lowered his son to the ground, Wiffle ball in hand. He put the boy down on the ground and approached me.

"Can I help you?" he asked.

Good sign. You don't say that if you're a criminal, right?

"Uh, yeah. Well, not help actually. Uh . . . I'm Darcy DeAngelis." I stopped for some reason, thinking my name would somehow jog his memory. I realized I had changed more than he had, and he wouldn't . . .

"What are you doing here?" he interrupted my thoughts. "Why are you bothering me?"

I had this feeling he knew who I was. "Do you know who I am?" I asked.

"I have an idea," he said. "Now what do you want?"

"Well, if you are the person who hit me . . ." I waited to see what he would do. He breathed in and crossed his arms. He was the one. I knew it. "I just wanted to tell you that it's okay and that I forgive you."

I said it so quickly I hardly heard it myself. Only the look in his eyes told me that I had gotten the words through. He squinted. He kicked the white landscaping stones at the end of the driveway. He looked down the street and then back at me. It seemed like forever before he spoke.

"You ought not to be here. Go home. I don't know what you expected, but the best thing, the only thing, for you to do is to forget me. Turn around and go home."

The words hit me hard. They were not like anything I thought I would hear. He didn't say he was sorry. He didn't ask how I was doing. He didn't say how badly he felt. He said nothing that would make this moment worthwhile. I felt stupid. I felt alone and cold. I really did want to leave, not just because he told me to. Tears started to form in my eyes.

And then he walked away. He went back through the front door of his house and closed it.

I stared at the house, tears continuing to build and then finally running down my face. I did not cry out. I just stared and let the warm tears trace my cheeks. *God, it wasn't supposed to happen this way. Mr. Germain was supposed to change, to realize what he had done, and to be relieved that I had forgiven him. What did I do to deserve this?* A feeling close to hatred and anger began to build in me. It was stopped short by a small voice.

"What's wrong?" The boy had walked up next to me without my seeing him.

"What?" I said.

"You're crying. Why?"

"Nothing. Really." I couldn't tell him what his dad

had done or why I was there. And I couldn't tell him how hurt I was.

"Okay." He paused. "Do you want to play catch?"

"No, I'd better get home. Thanks anyway." I turned away. Then a thought came to me. I turned back to the boy. "Do you like rocks?" I asked. "Like, do you have a favorite rock you keep in your room?"

He shook his head.

"Well, I've got something for you. It's a real special rock." I reached into my coat pocket and pulled out the Givestone. I blew the lint off and rubbed it between my fingers. I thought back to all that had happened in the last week. I remembered Eric's story, his dad's love, the forgiveness I had felt. I had thought I would hold on to the Givestone forever, but in that moment I realized there was something I had to do, something I wanted to do.

"Here," I said as I handed the stone to the boy. "It's really special. Keep it as a secret, okay. And then many years from now if there's ever someone who does something that hurts you, forgive them. And then give them this, okay?"

He nodded his head.

"Are you sure you understand?" I asked.

"Yep. I give it to someone when I forgive them."

"Yeah, you got it. Thanks." I turned away. "See ya." I headed down the street toward Chip, tears flowing freely again.

⁂

We caught the bus and got off near our block. It felt good to be in our own neighborhood. We traveled the remaining two blocks. The sun was low in the sky, and the shadows were long. It was cold, and the wind blew in our faces and cut through our winter coats. I tried making sense of what had happened by talking it out with Chip, but the hurt got in the way.

"Why was he so . . . cruel?" I asked. "It's as if I was the one who hit him instead of the other way around. Here I came all this way after so many years. And all I wanted to do was forgive him."

"Maybe he didn't want to be forgiven," Chip said.

"Why would anyone not want to be forgiven?" I almost yelled at Chip.

He didn't answer. He just walked beside me as my friend.

Ten

The year's first snow came two days after my meeting with Frank Germain. It was one of those snows with big, fat flakes that held their shape even after hitting the ground. They covered the grays and browns of November in less than an hour. Only the longest blades of grass poked through.

I had come home from school and was studying in the family room next to the fireplace when the snow began. The warmth of the fire and a deep sense of peace distracted me from my studies, but I didn't mind. I could always catch up on the homework tonight. For now, I wanted to enjoy the moment. Winter had come, and I wanted to enjoy its entrance for as long as possible.

My mom entered the room with cups of hot chocolate. "Mind if I join you?" she asked. She pulled up the rocking chair and sat next to me. We watched the flakes in silence together for a while.

Mom was the first to speak. "So how did your meeting with Mr. Germain go?"

I jumped visibly in my chair and almost spilled my cocoa. "How—how did you know?"

"Darcy, we know you. Once you get an idea in your head, you don't let go of it. And because your dad didn't tell you not to do it, I knew you'd follow through. How did you find him?"

"My friends and I tracked him down through the Internet."

"Darcy's gone high tech, huh?"

"Yeah. It was kind of fun tracking him down. I went to see him on Sunday with Chip." I paused. "But it really didn't turn out like I had imagined."

"Oh?"

"I thought it'd be like this really emotional reunion. Instead, I felt like I was intruding on his life. I cried afterward."

"What did he say?"

"Not much, really. He just didn't want to talk with me."

My mom nodded her head knowingly.

"But it's okay," I added. "I'm fine. I did what I wanted to do, and that was to tell him that I forgave him. I learned you can do that without the other person saying they're sorry. I don't know how he's feeling, but I know it's made a difference in me."

"Like you feel clean?"

"Yeah, kinda like that. Except it's more like there's nothing heavy pressing on me anymore."

"I know what you mean, I think." She paused, put down her mug, and sat forward in the rocking chair. "You know, Darcy, it was about six months after the accident that I spoke with Mr. Germain. He wasn't too happy then either. I was so angry with him that I probably frightened him. Maybe that's why he wasn't too interested in talking with you. It wasn't till about a year ago that I finally forgave him. What helped me do that was to realize that he didn't have control over what happened. You just flew out in front of him, and he couldn't stop in time. It was wrong for him to leave the scene, but I imagine he was really scared, too."

Outside, the last blades of grass gave up their fight against the snow, leaving the yard covered entirely in white. The light from our back porch came on as the evening sky grew dark. It caught the snow in mid-flight, drawing my attention to each flake's descent. It was hypnotizing, and the backyard scene below was captivating. As I looked out on the expanse of snow, I sighed.

"This is our first Christmas gift for the year, isn't it?" my mom said. "A quiet, peaceful gift."

I nodded.

But it wasn't the first, really. My heart had already received the gift of forgiveness. And I had passed it on. The snow would melt, and a hundred others would fall, but the peace of forgiveness would last forever.

Glossary

Here are a few words and expressions you met in *The Amazing Secret* that may have been new to you.

Accessible—A place that is easy to enter (steps and narrow doorways are a pain if you're in a wheelchair). Also, "accessible" to blind people may mean that there are Braille signs to help them find their way . . . like at an elevator. "Accessible" to a deaf person may mean that there is a sign language interpreter present or a TDD (telecommunication device for the deaf). The TDD allows a deaf person to type a message and send it over a phone line.

Paralyzed—A disabling condition in which parts of the body cannot move. Sometimes it means that the person cannot feel either. To be paralyzed does not mean that you are "stiff."

Physically challenged—A fancy way of saying that you are disabled or handicapped. Some people invent other phrases such as "motor impaired" or "handicapable" or "handicopable."

Pressure sore—A sore that occurs when a paralyzed person sits or lies in one position too long. It is very hard to heal, and disabled people take many precautions to prevent such sores from developing.

Ramp—Wheelchairs can't use steps! Also curb-cuts fit into this category.

A Note from Joni

I know you'd get a kick out of helping someone like my friend Darcy. She's pretty special, isn't she? Can you imagine yourself pushing her wheelchair or helping her transfer from one seat to another?

In case you are looking for ways to help a friend who is disabled, I've got a list of suggestions to share. Roll up your sleeves, reach out, and share God's love with a friend who is disabled. You'll not only put a smile on his or her face, you'll end up smiling, too.

Take some Windex or chrome cleaner, a rag, and a sponge, and shine up a friend's wheelchair. Grownups get their cars washed, waxed, and polished; why shouldn't kids in wheelchairs have a shiny set of wheels, too?

Learn how to push a wheelchair. There is more to it than simply throwing your weight behind the handlebars. Watch out for the cracks in the sidewalk or lips on the edge of the curb. Give a smooth, safe ride to a friend.

Offer to be a reacher or a picker-upper. Offer to reach for the top books on the library shelf or pick up an item for him on the way to class. How about carrying an extra load of books if they don't fit on your friend's lap? Look around and discover ways you can help.

When yakking with your friend in a wheelchair, be sure to stand in front and not off to the side or behind the chair. Then she won't have to constantly strain her neck to see you.

It's okay to ask your disabled friend about his handicapping condition, but remember that kids like to talk about lots of other things besides their chairs or crutches or hearing aids. They may enjoy discussing sports and games, TV shows, vacations, hobbies, and even homework—maybe!

Ask your disabled friend if she has any prayer requests. Sometimes kids, whether they're disabled or able-bodied, feel lonely, wish their parents didn't fight so much, need somebody to pray for them, or just want to talk.

Think ahead. If you're going to go somewhere with your disabled friend on the school campus, stop and think if there will be steps or a high curb. Will he be able to fit under the cafeteria table? If not, ask a teacher to help out. Remember, there is always a way if you've got the will!